Wait!
It's Friday

By Chris Barash • Illustrated by Christine Grove

APPLES & HONEY PRESS

To Marcie and Richie, who love Shabbat and know it's worth the wait.
—CB

For Molly and Gunnar
—CG

Apples & Honey Press
An imprint of Behrman House
Millburn, New Jersey 07041
www.applesandhoneypress.com

Text copyright © 2019 by Chris Barash
Illustrations copyright © 2019 by Christine Grove

ISBN 978-1-68115-542-5

Library of Congress Cataloging-in-Publication Data
Names: Barash, Chris, author. | Grove, Christine (Illustrator), illustrator.
Title: Wait! It's Friday / by Chris Barash ; illustrated by Christine Grove.
Other titles: Wait! It is Friday
Description: Millburn, New Jersey : Apples & Honey Press, an imprint of
   Behrman House, [2019] | Summary: A young boy eagerly awaits the start of
   Shabbat as challah rises, matzah balls cook, and the table is prepared by
   his loving familiy.
Identifiers: LCCN 2018008416 | ISBN 9781681155425
Subjects: | CYAC: Sabbath—Fiction. | Jews—United States—Fiction. | Family
   life—Fiction.
Classification: LCC PZ7.1.B3686 Wai 2018 | DDC [E]—dc23
LC record available at https://lccn.loc.gov/2018008416

Design by Anne Redmond
Edited by Dena Neusner
Art directed by Ann D. Koffsky
Printed in China

9 8 7 6 5 4 3 2 1

Today is Friday.

On Fridays I wait . . .

and wait . . .

and wait.

I wait with Daddy
   while the challah rises.

I wait with Nana
   while the matzah balls cook.

I wait with Helen
while the laundry gets done.

I wait with Daisy Dog
    while the flower man helps other customers.

I wait with Daddy
while he pays for our groceries.

Back at home, I wait with Sisi

while Mommy parks her car.

I wait with Uncle Bill
   while he drops coins into our tzedakah box.

I wait with my family
while the sun slips out of the sky.

But now the waiting
      is over:

the challah smells
      warm and
      sweet . . .

matzah balls float
      golden and
      fluffy . . .

the tablecloth
      lies fresh
      and crisp . . .

irises stand tall
      in a sparkly
      vase . . .

and candlelight makes wispy
shadows on the wall.

Shabbat is here.